Smithsonian Prehistoric Zone

Parasaurolophus

by Gerry Bailey
Illustrated by Gabe McIntosh

Crabtree Publishing Company

www.crabtreebooks.com

Crabtree Publishing Company

www.crabtreebooks.com

Author
Gerry Bailey

Illustrator
Gabe McIntosh

Editorial coordinator
Kathy Middleton

Editor
Lynn Peppas

Proofreader
Kathy Middleton

Prepress technician
Samara Parent

Print and production coordinator
Katherine Berti

Library of Congress Cataloging-in-Publication Data

Bailey, Gerry.
  Parasaurolophus / by Gerry Bailey ; illlustrated by Gabe McIntosh.
    p. cm. -- (Smithsonian prehistoric zone)
  Includes index.
  ISBN 978-0-7787-1812-3 (pbk. : alk. paper) -- ISBN 978-0-7787-1799-7 (reinforced library binding : alk. paper) -- ISBN 978-1-4271-9703-0 (electronic (pdf))
  1. Parasaurolophus--Juvenile literature. I. McIntosh, Gabe, ill. II. Title. III. Series.

QE862.O65B345 2011
567.914--dc22

                        2010044027

Library and Archives Canada Cataloguing in Publication

Bailey, Gerry
  Parasaurolophus / by Gerry Bailey ; illustrated
by Gabe McIntosh.

(Smithsonian prehistoric zone)
Includes index.
At head of title: Smithsonian Institution.
Issued also in electronic format.
ISBN 978-0-7787-1799-7 (bound).-- ISBN 978-0-7787-1812-3 (pbk.)

        1. Parasaurolophus--Juvenile literature.
I. McIntosh, Gabe II. Smithsonian Institution III. Title.
IV. Series: Bailey, Gerry. Smithsonian prehistoric zone.

QE862.O65B335 2011   j567.914   C2010-906884-X

Crabtree Publishing Company

www.crabtreebooks.com   1-800-387-7650
Copyright © **2011 CRABTREE PUBLISHING COMPANY**.
All rights reserved. No part of this publication may be reproduced, stored in a retrieval system or be transmitted in any form or by any means, electronic, mechanical, photocopying, recording, or otherwise, without the prior written permission of Crabtree Publishing Company. In Canada: we acknowledge the financial support of the Government of Canada through the Canada Book Fund for our publishing activities.

Published in the United States
Crabtree Publishing
PMB 59051
350 Fifth Avenue, 59th Floor
New York, New York 10118

Published in Canada
Crabtree Publishing
616 Welland Ave.
St. Catharines, Ontario
L2M 5V6

Printed in China/012011/GW20101014

Dinosaurs

Living things had been around for billions of years before dinosaurs came along. Animal life on Earth started with single-cell **organisms** that lived in the seas. About 380 million years ago, some animals came out of the sea and onto the land. These were the ancestors that would become the mighty dinosaurs.

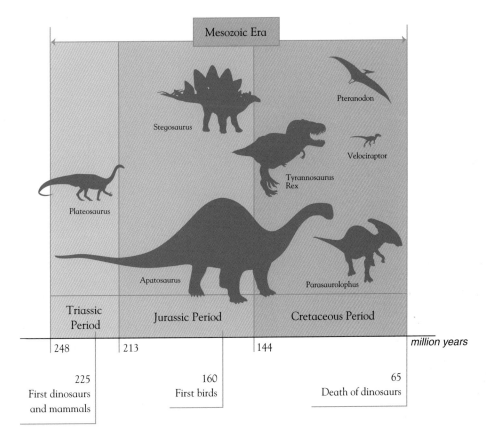

Mesozoic Era

Pteranodon

Stegosaurus

Velociraptor

Tyrannosaurus Rex

Plateosaurus

Apatosaurus

Parasaurolophus

Triassic Period	Jurassic Period	Cretaceous Period
248	213	144

million years

225
First dinosaurs and mammals

160
First birds

65
Death of dinosaurs

The dinosaur era is called the Mesozoic era. It is divided into three parts called the Triassic, Jurassic, and Cretaceous periods. During the Cretaceous period flowering plants grew for the first time. Plant-eating *hadrosaurs*, such as the *Parasaurolophus* and *Corythosaurus*, roamed the land. These were duck-billed dinosaurs. Meat-eaters, such as *Tyrannosaurus rex* and *Albertosaurus*, fed on the plant-eaters and other meat-eating reptiles. By the end of the Cretaceous period, dinosaurs (except birds) had been wiped out. No one is sure exactly why.

It was a misty early morning, 75 million years ago.
A strange-looking dinosaur with a swept-back crest
moved down to the river to drink and look for food.

This was a duck-billed dinosaur called
Parasaurolophus. He fed on the plants
that grew along the river bank.

Parasaurolophus looked around for tasty plants to eat as he splashed his way along the riverbank. He usually browsed while standing on all four legs, even though his front legs were shorter than his back ones.

This allowed him to get closer to the ferns and flowering plants he enjoyed. If he had to run fast to get away from a **predator**, he would rear up and run on just his hind legs.

Parasaurolophus was a **herbivore**. He liked
to eat stocky plants that looked like palms
called cycads. He ate ferns too. He used his
flattened beak to snip off the green leaves.

Rows of grinding teeth filled his cheeks. When these were worn out from chewing tough plants, new ones grew to replace them.

In his search for food Parasaurolophus had
strayed away from his herd and into the dark
forest. He rose up on his long back legs and
glanced around. He could be in danger here.

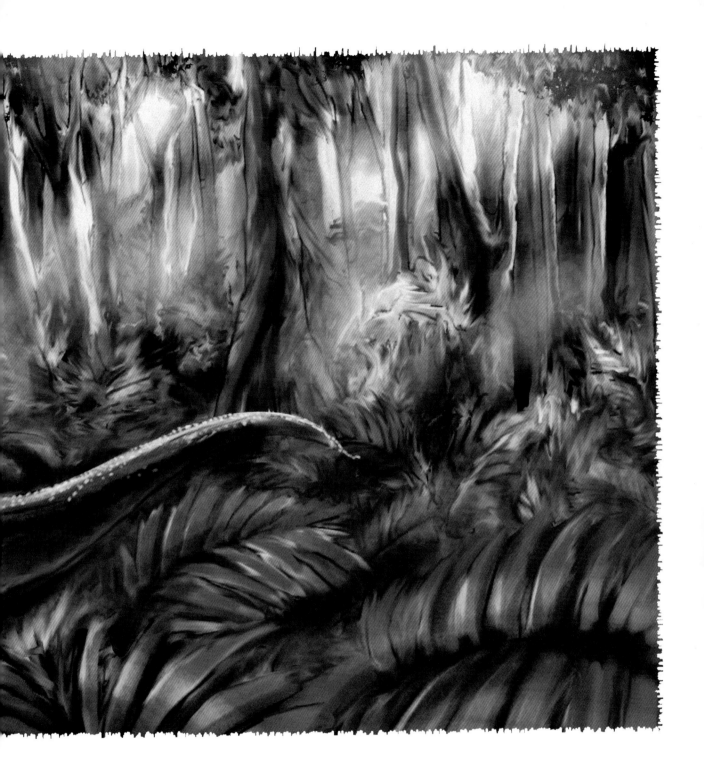

Parasaurolophus might be big but he had no
defense against a hungry **carnivore**, or meat-eater,
such as the huge Tyrannosaurus rex. Even smaller
carnivores, such as Struthiomimus, were a threat.

There were a lot of different sounds in the forest.
Parasaurolophus learned to recognize those sounds that
might mean danger. He heard a sound that warned
of another animal close by, and he looked around.

Luckily it was Styracosaurus.
It looked fearsome with its long
horns, but it was a plant-eater,
and so not a threat.

Danger was never far away when he was alone.
He had to get back to the river and his herd.
He began to run. He jumped over fallen logs.

He pushed branches out of his way with his front legs and crest. His large hipbones helped support the strong back leg muscles that gave him speed.

Parasaurolophus moved quickly between the trees. Suddenly he stopped. He smelled the air and knew he was not alone. He started off again, this time running faster. He sensed the gaping jaws and

terrible teeth of a predator closing in behind
him. A huge, meat-eating tyrannosaur called
Albertosaurus was chasing him. Parasaurolophus
was quick, but so was his enemy.

Suddenly Parasaurolophus raised his head.
He drew up air from his lungs and let out
a powerful, low bellow from his crest. The
strange sound stopped Albertosaurus briefly.

That gave Parasaurolophus just
enough time to run. He also knew
that the bellow would warn his herd
that danger was close by.

Parasaurolophus ran on tiptoe as fast as he could.
He kept his tail stuck out behind to help him balance.
He could not afford to fall over if he was to escape.

Albertosaurus was angry now and
chased as hard as he could. He wanted
Parasaurolophus for dinner.

Parasaurolophus reached the bank
of the river as Albertosaurus began
to catch up. He caught sight of the
rest of his herd.

The other dinosaurs started to run as Albertosaurus came up behind Parasaurolophus. Albertosaurus slowed down in the confusion. He had to decide which plant-eater to chase.

Knowing he might be safer in the
water, Parasaurolophus plunged
into the river. Albertosaurus did
not follow.

Unsure of what to do, he looked at one dinosaur then another as they disappeared across the river and into the forest beyond. Parasaurolophus looked back and knew he was safe. He would stay with the herd from now on.

All about Parasaurolophus

(pah-ruh-sore-OL-o-fus)

Parasaurolophus lived during the Cretaceous period between 76 and 74 million years ago. It was part of a group of dinosaurs called *hadrosaurs* that had flat, duckbill-shaped beaks at the end of their snouts. *Parasaurolophus* stood out because of the long crest on its head. The crests of male *Parasaurolophus* were longer than those of females.

Paleontologists are scientists who study **prehistoric** animals. They believe that the hollow crest was used to make sounds and gave the animal a greater sense of smell. It also helped the dinosaurs recognize their **species** and attract a mate. Male dinosaurs probably made deeper, louder sounds than the females.

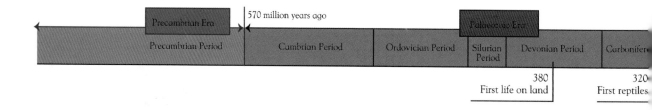

570 million years ago

Precambrian Era		Palaeozoic Era				
Precambrian Period	Cambrian Period	Ordovician Period	Silurian Period	Devonian Period	Carbonifer
				380 First life on land	320 First reptiles

In order to break down plant material, *Parasaurolophus* had rows of leaf-shaped teeth in its cheeks. These teeth were used to grind down the food they had plucked from plants. Food included pine needles, leaves, and twigs.

		248				65		Now
				Mesozoic Era			Cenozoic Era	
eriod	Permian Period	Triassic Period	Jurassic Period	Cretaceous Period				

1.8
First humans

Duck bills

Parasaurolophus belonged to a group of duck-billed dinosaurs called *hadrosaurs*. Most likely, they started out living in central Asia but by the end of the Cretaceous period had moved into most parts of the **northern hemisphere**. They survived for many millions of years and became the most common kind of plant-eater of late Cretaceous times. This was certainly because they ate a whole variety of different plants, which helped them survive when the climate became drier.

Hadrosaurs had a broad, flattened snout with a toothless beak that looked a little like a duck's bill. It used its beak to pluck leaves and fruit from plants. There were no teeth in the front of its mouth, but there were rows of cheek teeth in its upper and lower jaws. When the teeth wore out, new ones replaced them.

Although they came from the same group, different *hadrosaur* types often looked unalike. Some, such as *Saurolophus*, may have had an **inflatable** nose sac that it used to communicate with by hooting. Others, such as *Corythosaurus* and *Parasaurolophus*, had a variety of crests that acted as **echo chambers**. They could produce low bellowing sounds to call to *hadrosaurs* of the same type.

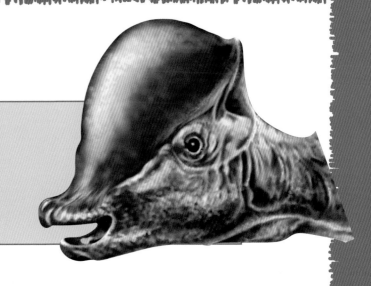

Saurolophus may have had an inflatable sac supported by its crest that it may have blown up to make sounds.

Corythosaurus had a crest like a kind of helmet, which contained tubes from its **nasal passages**. It probably used them to make loud low-pitched sounds.

The male *Parasaurolophus* had a longer crest than the female.

What exactly was it for?

For many years scientists have been wondering what the crest on the head of the duck-billed dinosaur *Parasaurolophus* was actually for. Some suggested it was just for **display**. This way dinosaurs could recognize other members of their pack or attract a mate. Others thought it might be used to give the animals a better sense of smell because it was linked to their nasal passages. A third idea was that the dinosaurs used their crests to create a kind of sound. This sound might help them attract a mate or **communicate** with other dinosaurs.

Scientists carried out a scan of a *hadrosaur* (duck-billed dinosaur) skull. This helped them build a picture of what the brain and crest may have looked like. The scan showed that the part of the brain used for smelling was small and not well **developed**. So the crest was probably not used as a smelling aid. The part of the brain used for communication was found to be larger. Computer models showed that the crest could be used to make a strange, low-**frequency** sound. The scan also showed a delicate **inner ear** that could pick up this kind of sound.

Parasaurolophus probably used its crest to make sounds that would attract others in the group or give out a warning if danger was near.

Glossary

carnivore A meat-eater that feeds on another animal's flesh

communicate To talk or share information with another

develop To grow

display To show something to others

echo chamber An enclosed space that makes the same sound two or more times because the sound bounces off the surface and comes back

frequency The number of times per second that something vibrates such as sound

herbivore A plant-eating animal

inflatable Able to be filled with air or other gases

inner ear The part of the ear inside the skull that controls hearing and balance

nasal passage The inside walls of the nose that move air in and out, and are responsible for smell

northern hemisphere The half of Earth found north of the equator

organism A form of life

predator An animal that hunts other animals for food

prehistoric Belonging to a time before history was being written down

species Animals that are grouped together because they have similar characteristics

Index

Further Reading and Websites

Parasaurolophus and Other Duck-billed and Beaked Herbivores by David West. Gareth Stevens Publishing (2010)

Hadrosaurs: The Duck-billed Dinosaur by Rob Shone. PowerKids Press (2009)

Websites:

www.smithsonianeducation.org